Emma and Muse

words and pictures by
Nancy Lemon

Albert Whitman & Company
Chicago, Illinois

Emma's most favorite thing in the world to draw was dogs...
well, one dog in particular. Muse. Most days, she could be
found doing just that...

and when she wasn't drawing Muse, she painted his portrait...

or she sculpted him out of clay.

Emma experimented with many different kinds of
mediums to capture her dog exactly right.

She was an artist, and all of her art was inspired by her Muse.

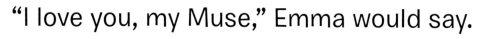

"I love you, my Muse," Emma would say.

"You are why I am an artist."

"Woof, woof, woof!" Muse barked lovingly.

One afternoon as Emma prepared a large canvas for
her next masterpiece,

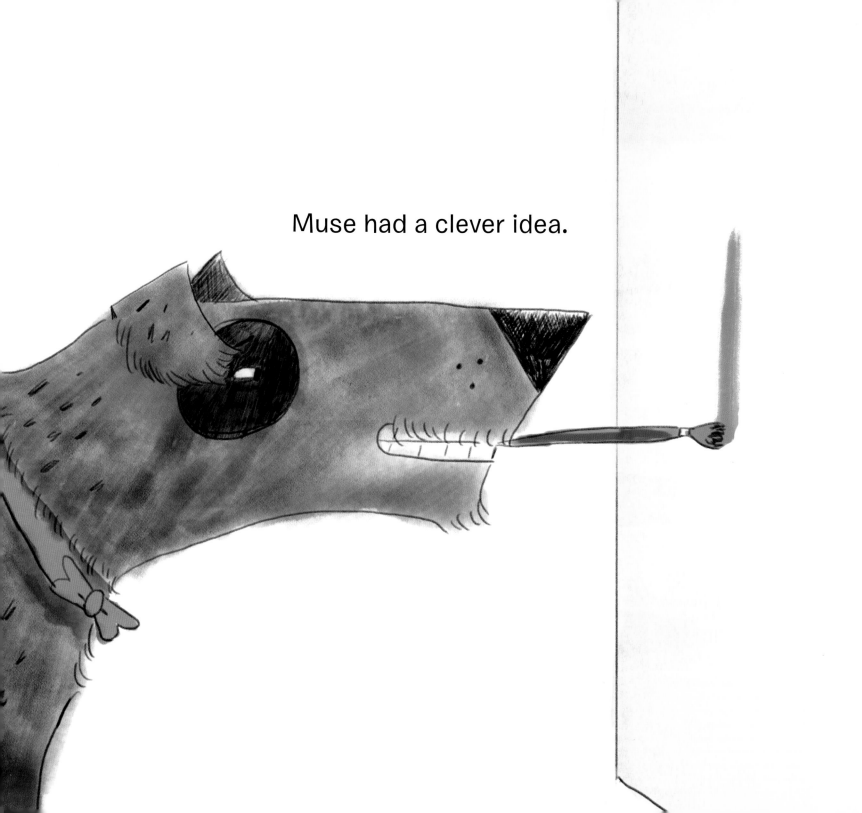

Muse had a clever idea.

"NO! STOP, MUSE! NO!!!"

"BAD DOG, MUSE! NO, BAD BOY!!" Emma shouted.

Brokenhearted, Muse decided to leave home.

With Muse gone, Emma just couldn't find the right
thing to draw or paint. Her mind was a blank canvas.

Emma was angry that Muse had messed with her work, so she tried to draw her anger. Emma was sad that Muse had left, so she tried to paint her sadness. She was worried that Muse had left forever and tried to sculpt her worry.

It was no use.

Emma was not inspired,
just sad and lonely. First she
had lost Muse. Now had she
lost her creative juices too?

Emma thought she should clear her head, so she tried her hand at something new: a still life. The good thing about plants was that they couldn't paint on your canvases, and they couldn't run away from home...

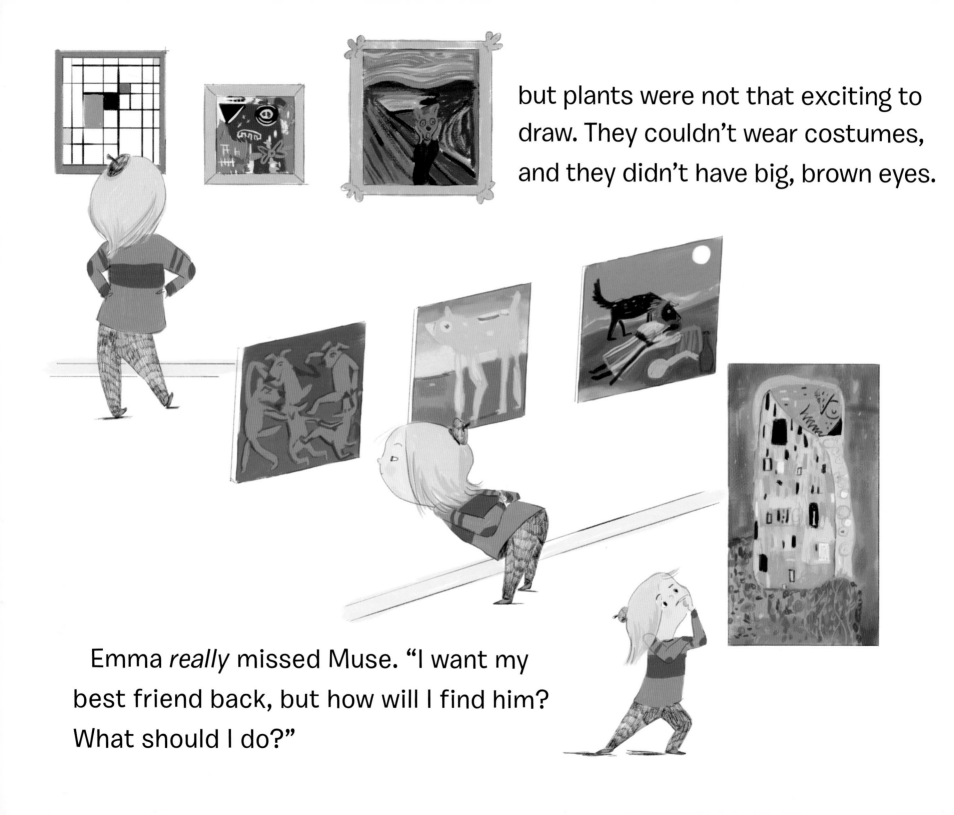

but plants were not that exciting to draw. They couldn't wear costumes, and they didn't have big, brown eyes.

Emma *really* missed Muse. "I want my best friend back, but how will I find him? What should I do?"

Then a creative spark hit her like lightning, and she got a BIG, artsy idea.

She didn't have to paint plants! She could paint apologies!

She would post her paintings on every city wall
and hope that Muse would see it.

While Emma plastered the city with her posters, Muse was sniffing out new collaborators at a festival in the park.

Maybe he could find an artistic friend here, he thought as he gazed at different paintings. But no one could draw a dog like Emma.

"Well, hello there, dog," said an artsy-looking lady who held out a treat.

"Hey, I recognize you! You're the dog on all the giant posters. Look at that, Muse. Someone really misses you."

Muse gazed at the posters of himself and barked a happy bark. He didn't *really* want a new artist—he wanted Emma! And he set out to find his way home.

"MUSE! I thought I had lost you forever!!" said Emma between doggy kisses. "I'm SO sorry I yelled at you!"

And for their next collaboration, Emma insisted
Muse add his finishing touches.

Glossary of Art Terms

artsy: being artistic or interested in art

canvas: a strong, rough cloth used in painting

collaboration: working with someone to create something (like art!)

creativity: the use of the imagination, especially in the making of an artistic work

experimenting: trying out new ways of creating

masterpiece: an outstanding work of art

mediums: materials, such as paint, graphite, ink, pastel, and clay, used to create a work of art

muse: an artist's inspiration for creating

still life: a painting or drawing of an arrangement of objects

To my Matt, my lifetime collaborator, and to Rosalee, my original Muse

Library of Congress Cataloging-in-Publication Data
Names: Lemon, Nancy, author, illustrator.
Title: Emma and Muse / Nancy Lemon.
Description: Chicago, Illinois: Albert Whitman and Company, 2018.
Summary: Artist Emma scolds her dog, Muse, for changing one of her paintings but when
he leaves, so does her creativity until she finds a special way to bring him home.
Identifiers: LCCN 2017041022 | ISBN 978-0-8075-1994-3 (hardcover)
Subjects: | CYAC: Artists—Fiction. | Dogs—Fiction. | Human-animal relationships—Fiction.
BISAC: JUVENILE FICTION / Animals / Dogs. | JUVENILE FICTION / Art & Architecture. | JUVENILE FICTION / Social Issues / Friendship.
Classification: LCC PZ7.1.L4458 Emm 2018 | DDC [E]—dc23
LC record available at https://lccn.loc.gov/2017041022

Printed in China
10 9 8 7 6 5 4 3 2 1 HH 22 21 20 19 18 17
Design by Jordan Kost and Morgan Beck

For more information about Albert Whitman & Company,
visit our website at www.albertwhitman.com.

E LEMON   FLT
Lemon, Nancy,
Emma and Muse /

06/18